D1473658

TRANSFORMERS
DARK OF THE MOON
FOUNDATION

VOLUME 3

STORY BY JOHN BARBER
ART BY ANDREW GRIFFITH

COLORS BY PRISCILLA TRAMONTANO
LETTERS BY CHRIS MOWRY AND SHAWN LEE
SERIES ASSISTANT EDITOR CARLOS GUZMAN
SERIES EDITOR ANDY SCHMIDT
COLLECTION EDITOR JUSTIN EISINGER
COLLECTION DESIGNER SHAWN LEE

Licensed By:
GM Hasbro Paramount IDW Spotlight

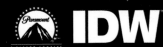

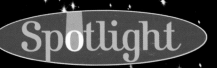

visit us at www.abdopublishing.com

Reinforced library bound edition published in 2012 by Spotlight,
a division of the ABDO Group, PO Box 398166, Minneapolis, MN 55439.
Spotlight produces high-quality reinforced library bound editions for schools and
libraries. Published by agreement with IDW Publishing. www.idwpublishing.com

Printed in the United States of America, North Mankato, Minnesota.
102011
012012
♻ This book contains at least 10% recycled materials.

Library of Congress Cataloging-in-Publication Data

Barber, John, 1976-
 Transformers, dark of the moon movie prequel / story by John Barber ; art by
Andrew Griffith ; colors by Priscilla Tramontano ; letters by Chris Mowry.
   p. cm. -- (Dark of the moon: foundation ; v. 4)
  ISBN 978-1-59961-971-2 (volume 1) -- ISBN 978-1-59961-972-9 (volume 2) --
ISBN 978-1-59961-973-6 (volume 3) -- ISBN 978-1-59961-974-3 (volume 4)
 1. Graphic novels. I. Griffith, Andrew, 1976- ill. II. Transformers, dark of the moon
(Motion picture) III. Title. IV. Title: Dark of the moon movie prequel.
 PZ7.7.B35Tr 2012
 741.5'973--dc23
                          2011029052

All Spotlight books are reinforced library binding
and manufactured in the United States of America.

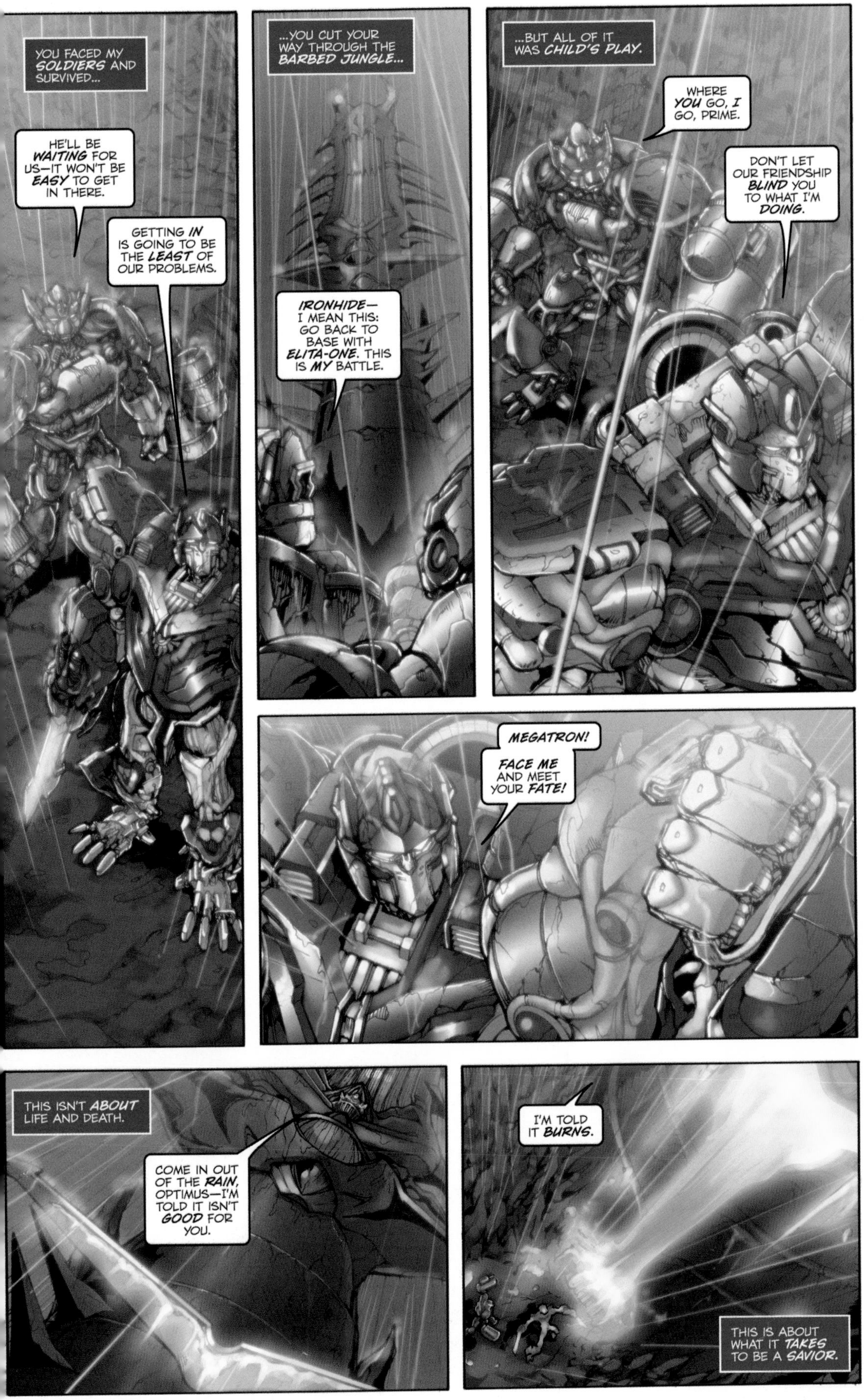
YOU FACED MY SOLDIERS AND SURVIVED...
HE'LL BE WAITING FOR US—IT WON'T BE EASY TO GET IN THERE.
GETTING IN IS GOING TO BE THE LEAST OF OUR PROBLEMS.
...YOU CUT YOUR WAY THROUGH THE BARBED JUNGLE...
IRONHIDE— I MEAN THIS: GO BACK TO BASE WITH ELITA-ONE. THIS IS MY BATTLE.
...BUT ALL OF IT WAS CHILD'S PLAY.
WHERE YOU GO, I GO, PRIME.
DON'T LET OUR FRIENDSHIP BLIND YOU TO WHAT I'M DOING.
MEGATRON!
FACE ME AND MEET YOUR FATE!
THIS ISN'T ABOUT LIFE AND DEATH.
COME IN OUT OF THE RAIN, OPTIMUS—I'M TOLD IT ISN'T GOOD FOR YOU.
I'M TOLD IT BURNS.
THIS IS ABOUT WHAT IT TAKES TO BE A SAVIOR.

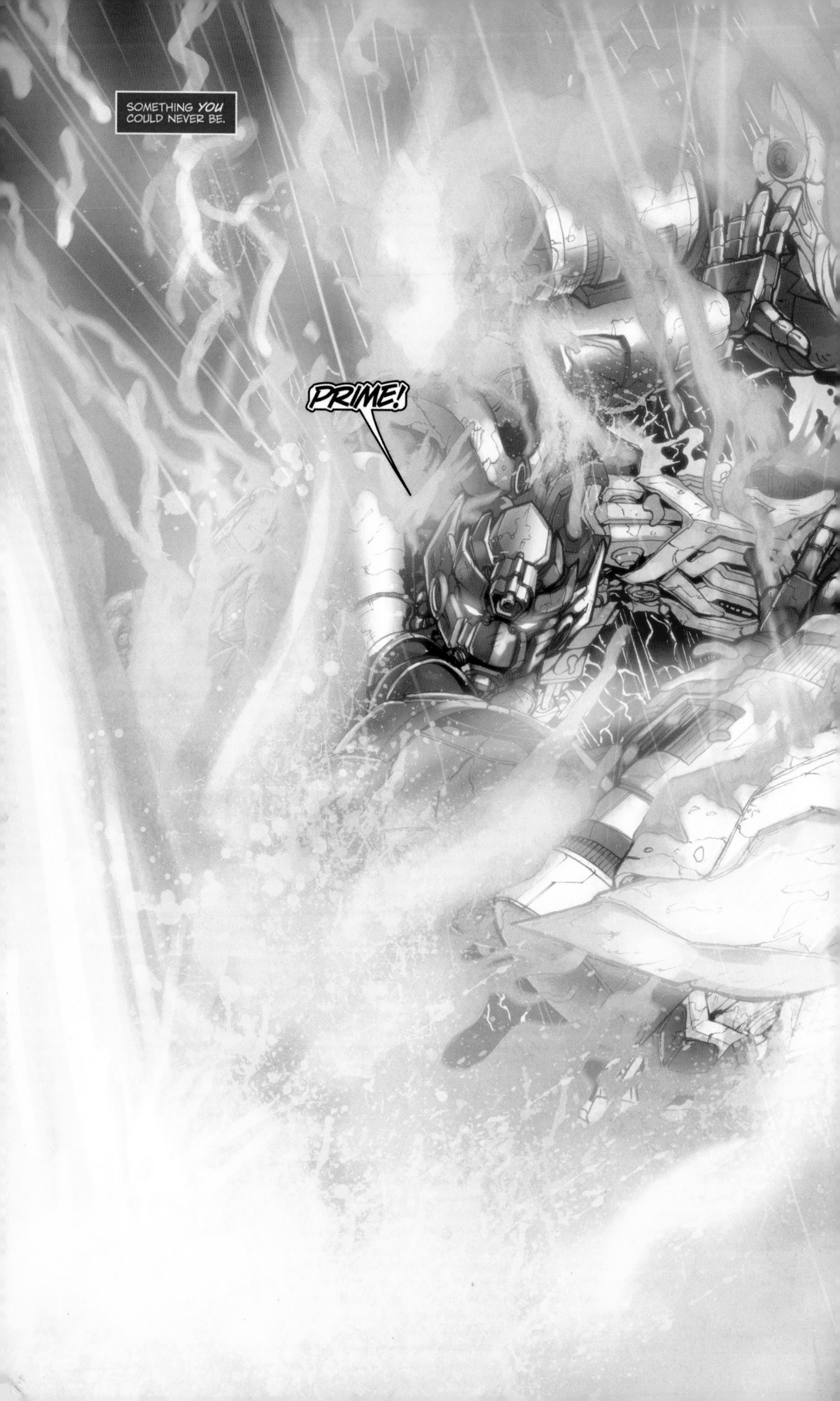
SOMETHING *YOU* COULD NEVER BE.
PRIME!

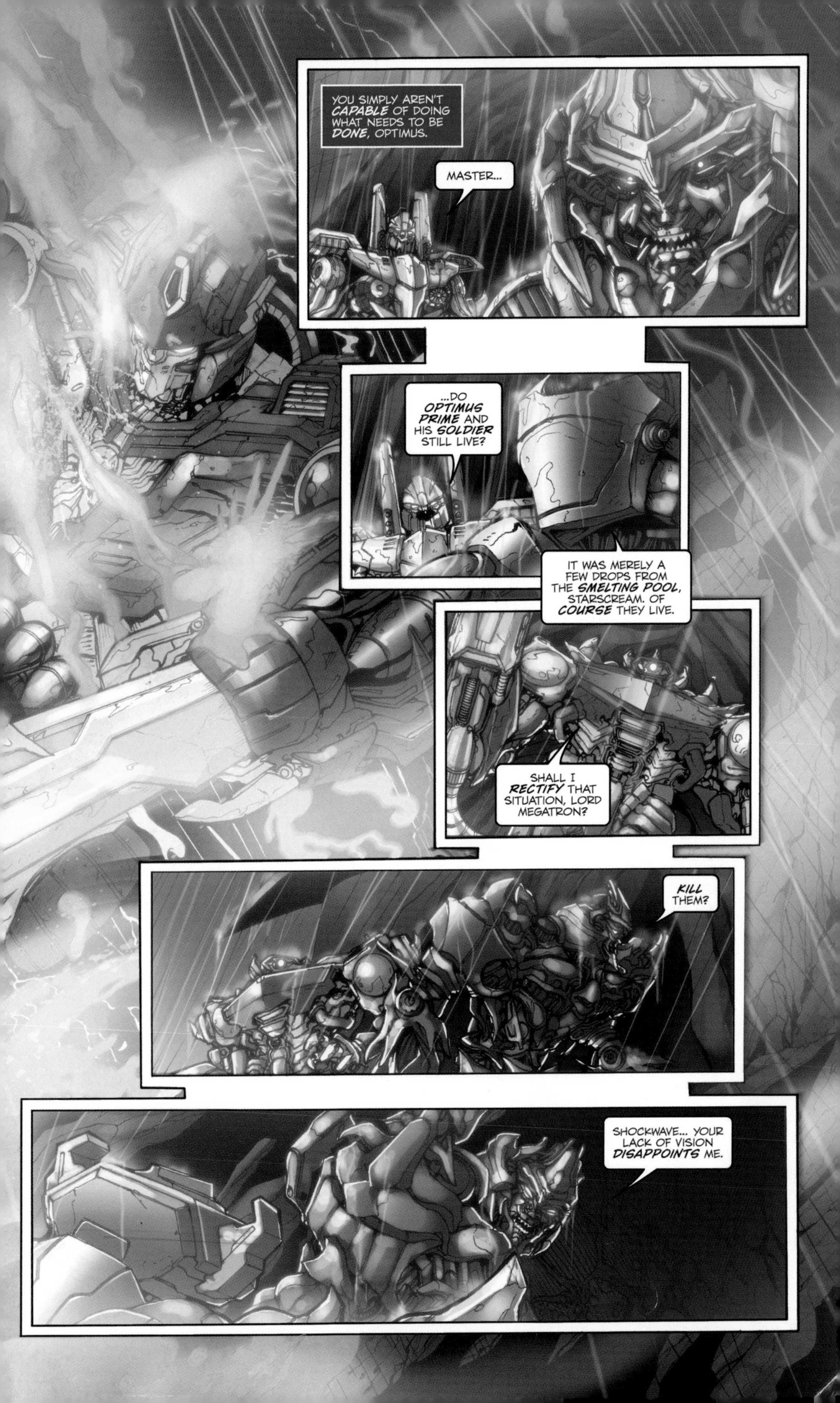

YOU SIMPLY AREN'T CAPABLE OF DOING WHAT NEEDS TO BE DONE, OPTIMUS.
MASTER...
...DO OPTIMUS PRIME AND HIS SOLDIER STILL LIVE?
IT WAS MERELY A FEW DROPS FROM THE SMELTING POOL, STARSCREAM. OF COURSE THEY LIVE.
SHALL I RECTIFY THAT SITUATION, LORD MEGATRON?
KILL THEM?
SHOCKWAVE... YOUR LACK OF VISION DISAPPOINTS ME.

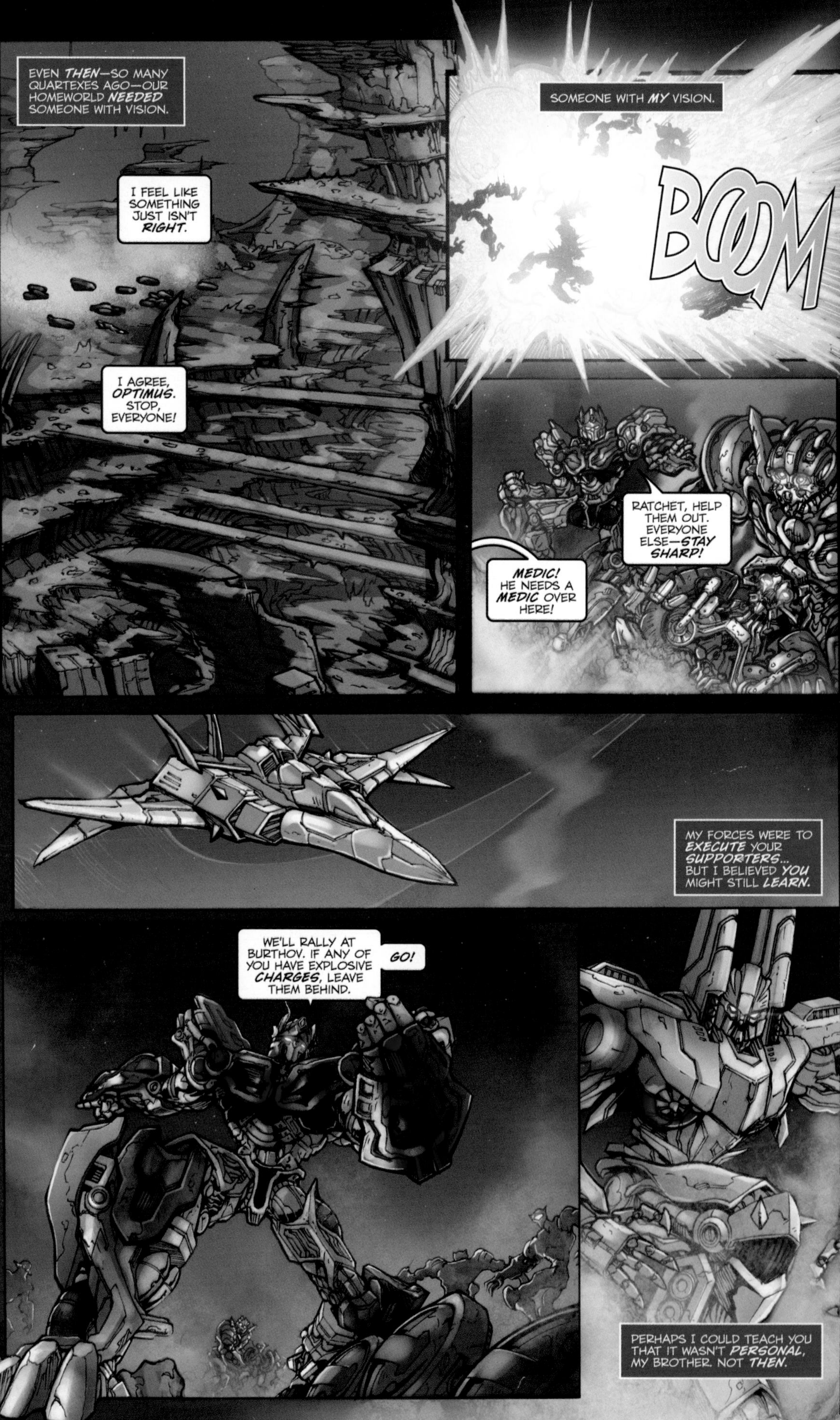
EVEN THEN—SO MANY QUARTEXES AGO—OUR HOMEWORLD NEEDED SOMEONE WITH VISION.
I FEEL LIKE SOMETHING JUST ISN'T RIGHT.
I AGREE, OPTIMUS. STOP, EVERYONE!
SOMEONE WITH MY VISION.
BOOM
RATCHET, HELP THEM OUT. EVERYONE ELSE—STAY SHARP!
MEDIC! HE NEEDS A MEDIC OVER HERE!
MY FORCES WERE TO EXECUTE YOUR SUPPORTERS... BUT I BELIEVED YOU MIGHT STILL LEARN.
WE'LL RALLY AT BURTHOV. IF ANY OF YOU HAVE EXPLOSIVE CHARGES, LEAVE THEM BEHIND.
GO!
PERHAPS I COULD TEACH YOU THAT IT WASN'T PERSONAL, MY BROTHER. NOT THEN.

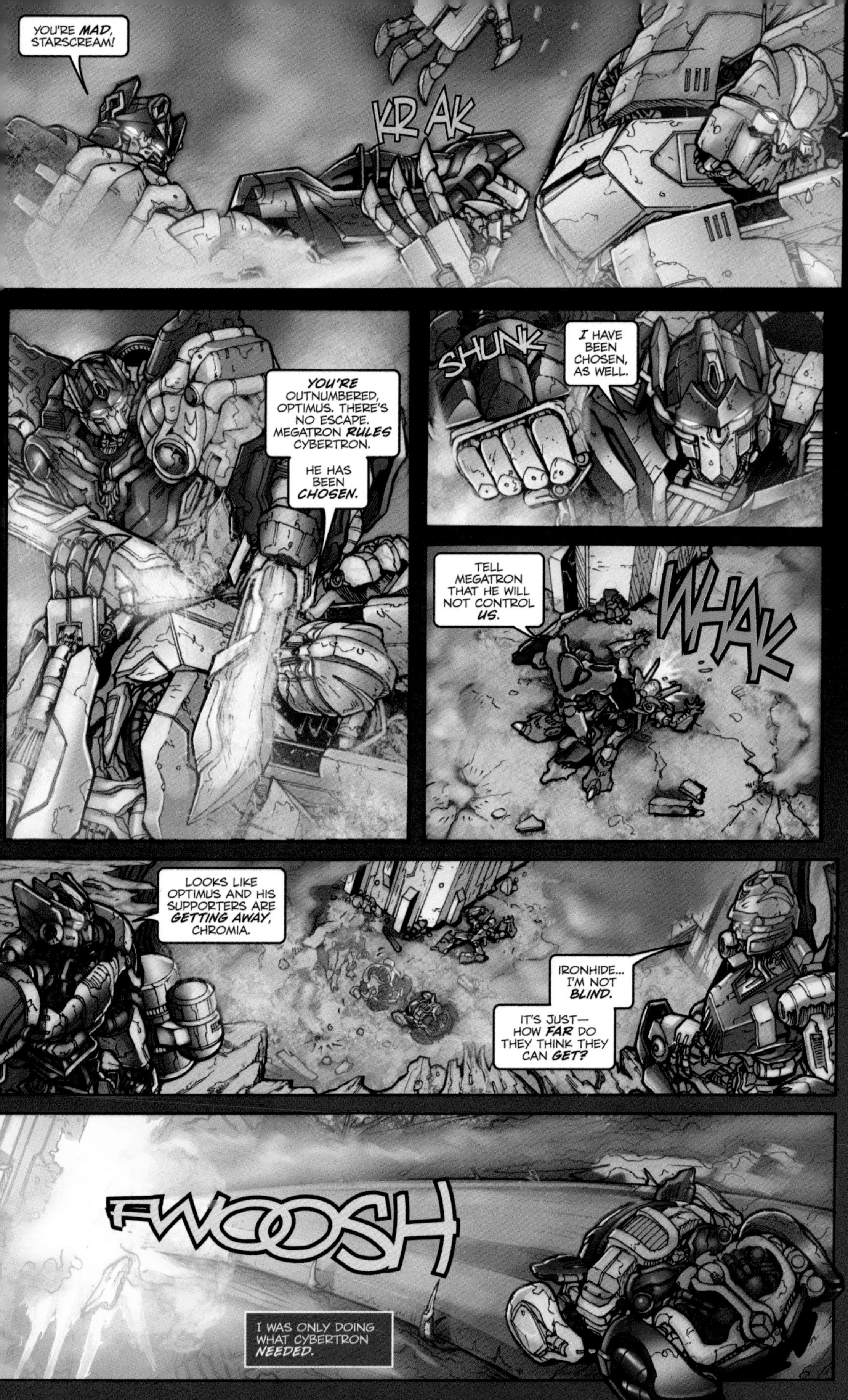
YOU'RE MAD, STARSCREAM!
KRAK
YOU'RE OUTNUMBERED, OPTIMUS. THERE'S NO ESCAPE. MEGATRON RULES CYBERTRON.
HE HAS BEEN CHOSEN.
SHUNK
I HAVE BEEN CHOSEN, AS WELL.
TELL MEGATRON THAT HE WILL NOT CONTROL US.
WHAK
LOOKS LIKE OPTIMUS AND HIS SUPPORTERS ARE GETTING AWAY, CHROMIA.
IRONHIDE... I'M NOT BLIND.
IT'S JUST— HOW FAR DO THEY THINK THEY CAN GET?
FWOOSH
I WAS ONLY DOING WHAT CYBERTRON NEEDED.

FREEDOM HAD MADE US WEAK.

THERE WAS A UNIVERSE, JUST OUTSIDE OUR GRASP, WAITING TO BE REMADE IN OUR IMAGE.

IN MY IMAGE.

JOIN ME!

PLEDGE YOUR ALLEGIANCE TO YOUR NEW LEADER! PLEDGE YOUR ALLEGIANCE TO YOUR NEW NAME... FOR THOSE WHO SIDE WITH ME SHALL BE KNOWN AS—

—DECEPTICONS!

AS ALL WHO STAND AGAINST US FALL BENEATH THE IRON HEEL OF THE DECEPTICON EMPIRE...

...LET THE TRAITORS OF OUR OWN RACE BE CRUSHED FIRST.

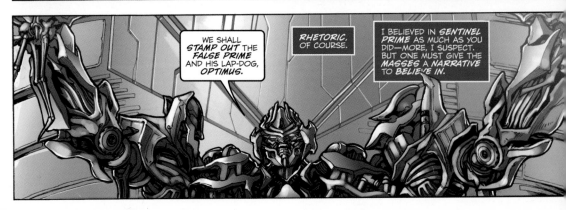

WE SHALL STAMP OUT THE FALSE PRIME AND HIS LAP-DOG, OPTIMUS.

RHETORIC, OF COURSE.

I BELIEVED IN SENTINEL PRIME AS MUCH AS YOU DID—MORE, I SUSPECT. BUT ONE MUST GIVE THE MASSES A NARRATIVE TO BELIEVE IN.

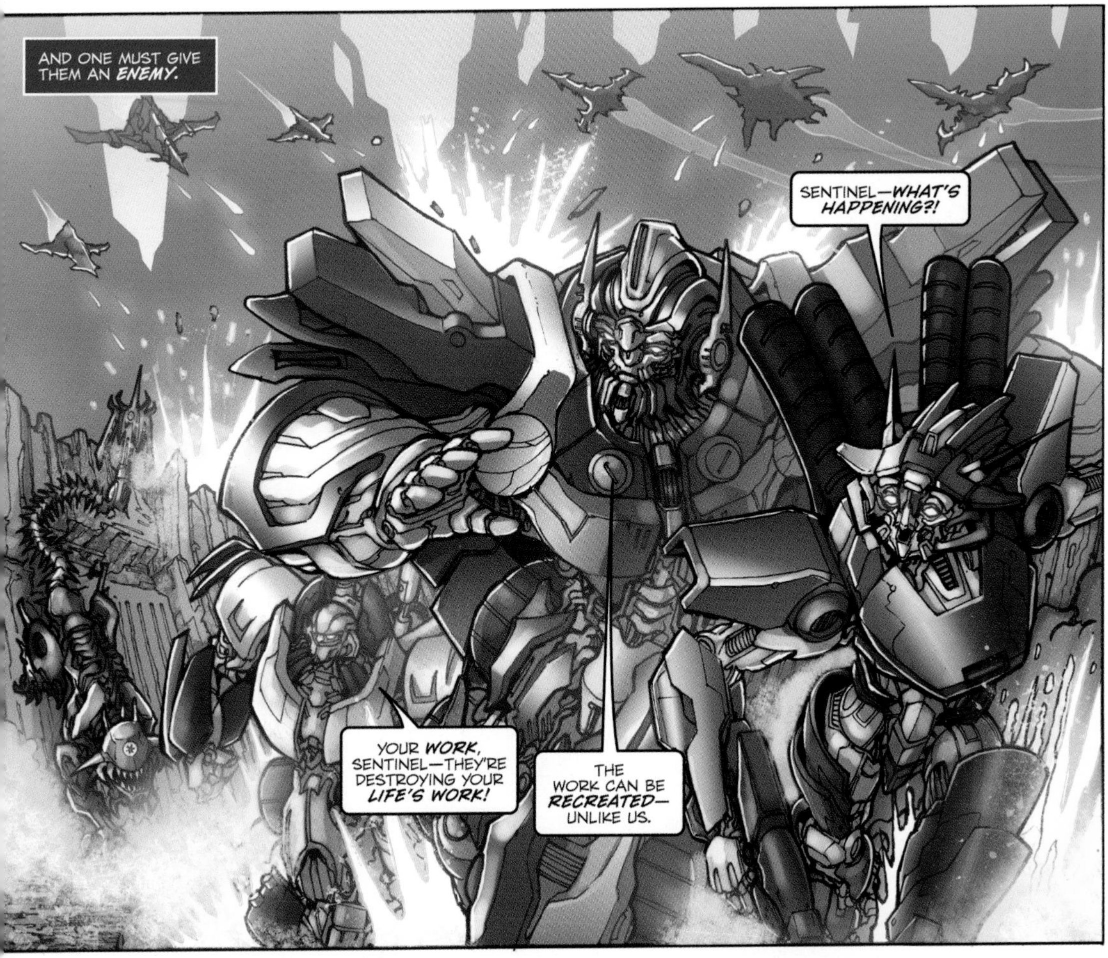
AND ONE MUST GIVE THEM AN *ENEMY.*
SENTINEL—*WHAT'S HAPPENING?!*
YOUR *WORK*, SENTINEL—THEY'RE DESTROYING YOUR *LIFE'S WORK!*
THE WORK CAN BE *RECREATED*—UNLIKE US.

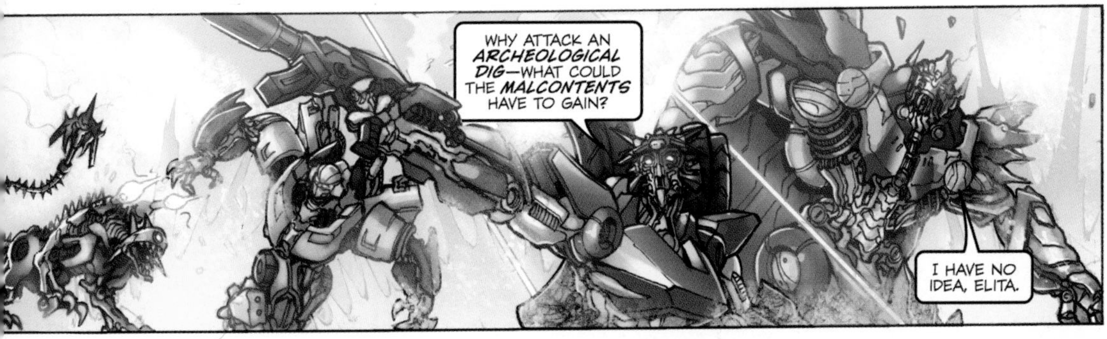
WHY ATTACK AN *ARCHEOLOGICAL DIG*—WHAT COULD THE *MALCONTENTS* HAVE TO GAIN?
I HAVE NO IDEA, ELITA.

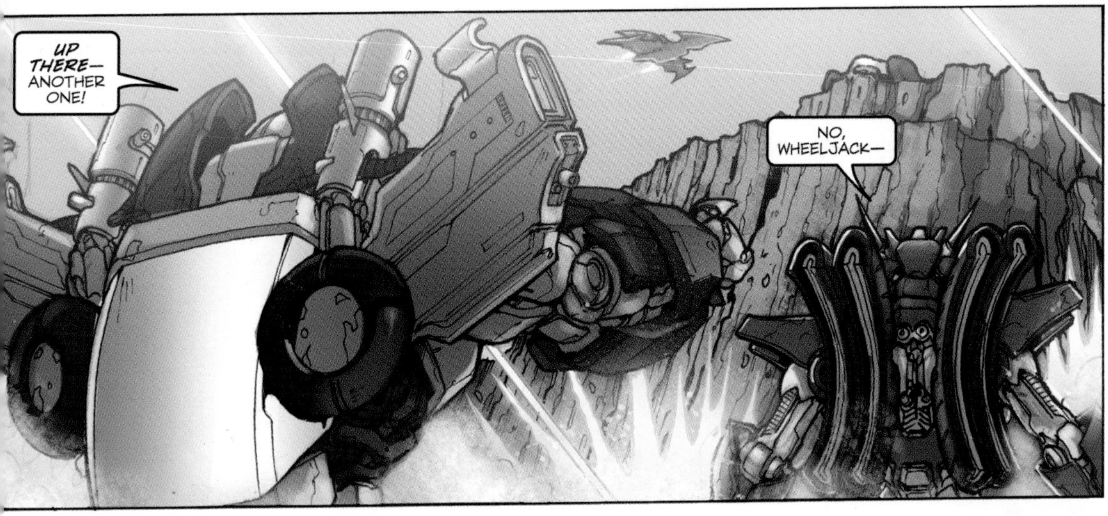
UP THERE—ANOTHER ONE!
NO, WHEELJACK—

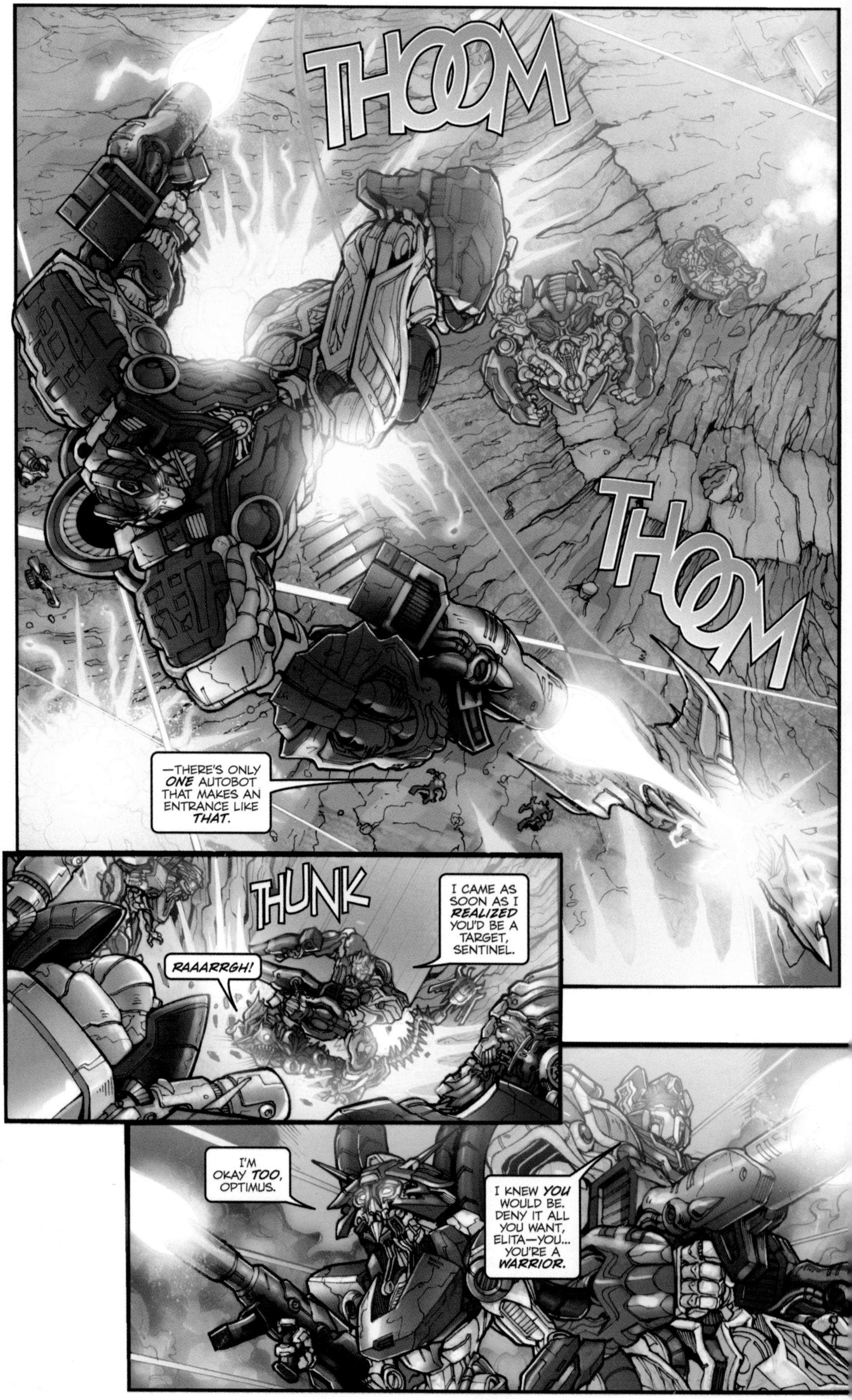
THOOM
THOOM
—THERE'S ONLY ONE AUTOBOT THAT MAKES AN ENTRANCE LIKE THAT.
THUNK
I CAME AS SOON AS I REALIZED YOU'D BE A TARGET, SENTINEL.
RAAARRGH!
I'M OKAY TOO, OPTIMUS.
I KNEW YOU WOULD BE. DENY IT ALL YOU WANT, ELITA—YOU... YOU'RE A WARRIOR.

I'M COMMITTED TO *PEACE*, BUT IF I HAVE TO *FORCE* THESE *MALCONTENTS* AWAY...

THAT'S *NOT* WHO'S BEHIND THIS. *MEGATRON* HAS DECLARED WAR.

WAR? AGAINST *WHOM*?

AGAINST ALL WHO STAND FOR *FREEDOM*.

ARCEE—

SHE'S *FINE*. WE GOT AWAY WHEN MEGATRON'S FORCES TRIED TO *DETAIN* US. BUT *CHROMIA*...

MY OWN *SISTER*— SIDING WITH *MEGATRON*?

I DIDN'T—

HALT, TRAITORS!

BY ORDERS OF *LORD MEGATRON*, YOU ARE FOUND GUILTY OF *SEDITION* AND SENTENCED TO *IMMEDIATE EXECUTION*, SENTINEL PRIME.

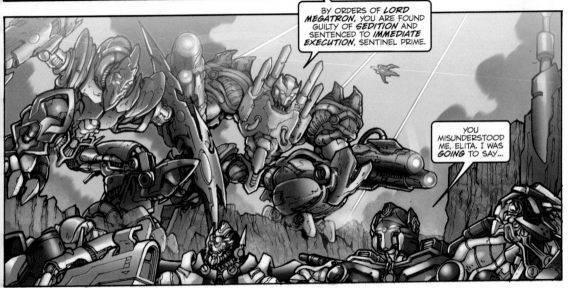

YOU *MISUNDERSTOOD* ME, ELITA. I WAS *GOING* TO SAY...

UK!

UT!

SHZAAKKK

SHZAAKKK

...CHROMIA IS RIGHT *BEHIND* ME.

WE'VE GOT TO GET *OUT* OF HERE.

WHAT IS GOING *ON?!*

I WAS *HELD UP* CUTTING MY WAY THROUGH THESE BUTCHERS. SORRY FOR THE DRAMATIC ENTRANCE.

I WISH I COULD'VE GOTTEN HERE *EARLIER*, SAVED SOME... SOME MORE...

IT'S *OKAY*, CHROMIA.

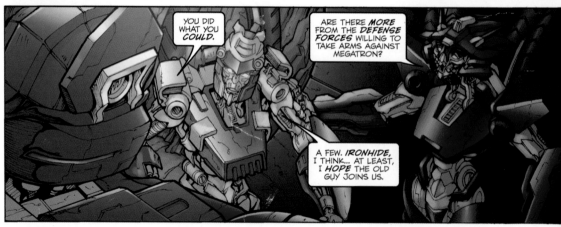

YOU DID WHAT YOU *COULD*.

ARE THERE *MORE* FROM THE *DEFENSE FORCES* WILLING TO TAKE ARMS AGAINST MEGATRON?

A FEW. *IRONHIDE*, I THINK... AT LEAST, I *HOPE* THE OLD GUY JOINS US.

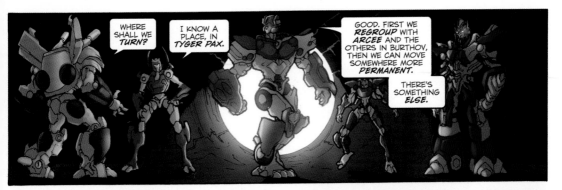

WHERE SHALL WE *TURN?*

I KNOW A PLACE, IN *TYGER PAX.*

GOOD. FIRST WE *REGROUP* WITH *ARCEE* AND THE OTHERS IN BURTHOV, THEN WE CAN MOVE SOMEWHERE MORE *PERMANENT.*

THERE'S SOMETHING *ELSE.*

THIS *MARKING* ON MY HELMET— ARCEE FOUND THE SAME SYMBOL AMONG SOME *ARTIFACTS* WE'D DUG UP.

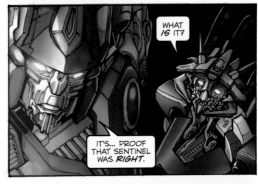

WHAT *IS* IT?

IT'S... PROOF THAT SENTINEL WAS *RIGHT.*

IT'S THE *SYMBOL* OF THE *PRIMES.*

IT HAS ALWAYS BEEN YOUR *NATURE* TO NEED *UNASSAILABLE FACTS* IN ORDER TO *ACCEPT* THE TRUTH.

AND NOW I *DO* ACCEPT IT. LIKE YOU, I AM A *PRIME.*

WHAT DOES THAT *MEAN,* OPTIMUS?

IT MEANS *TROUBLE.*

DO NOT THINK ME *UNGRATEFUL.*

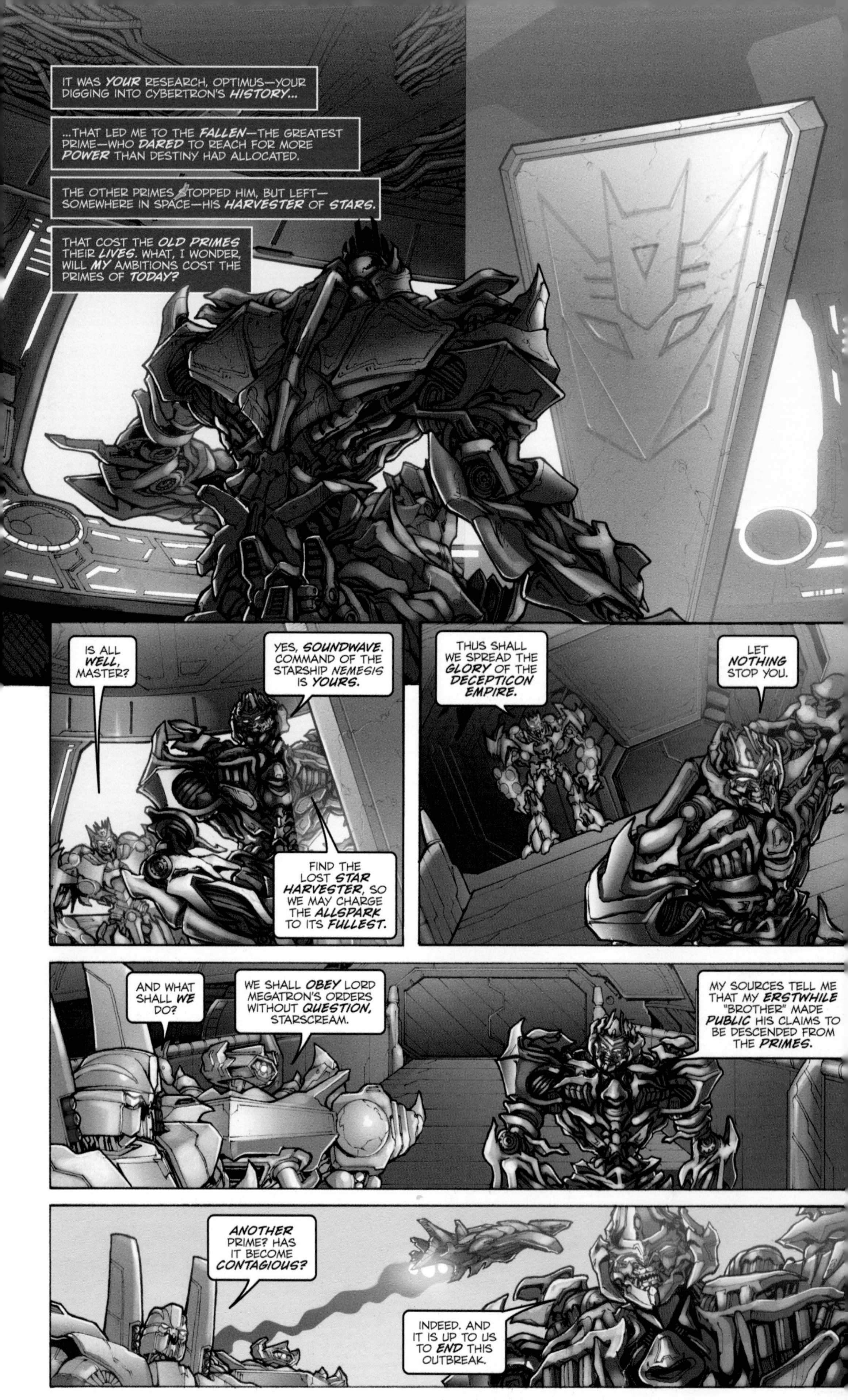
IT WAS YOUR RESEARCH, OPTIMUS—YOUR DIGGING INTO CYBERTRON'S HISTORY...
...THAT LED ME TO THE FALLEN—THE GREATEST PRIME—WHO DARED TO REACH FOR MORE POWER THAN DESTINY HAD ALLOCATED.
THE OTHER PRIMES STOPPED HIM, BUT LEFT—SOMEWHERE IN SPACE—HIS HARVESTER OF STARS.
THAT COST THE OLD PRIMES THEIR LIVES. WHAT, I WONDER, WILL MY AMBITIONS COST THE PRIMES OF TODAY?
IS ALL WELL, MASTER?
YES, SOUNDWAVE. COMMAND OF THE STARSHIP NEMESIS IS YOURS.
FIND THE LOST STAR HARVESTER, SO WE MAY CHARGE THE ALLSPARK TO ITS FULLEST.
THUS SHALL WE SPREAD THE GLORY OF THE DECEPTICON EMPIRE.
LET NOTHING STOP YOU.
AND WHAT SHALL WE DO?
WE SHALL OBEY LORD MEGATRON'S ORDERS WITHOUT QUESTION, STARSCREAM.
MY SOURCES TELL ME THAT MY ERSTWHILE "BROTHER" MADE PUBLIC HIS CLAIMS TO BE DESCENDED FROM THE PRIMES.
ANOTHER PRIME? HAS IT BECOME CONTAGIOUS?
INDEED. AND IT IS UP TO US TO END THIS OUTBREAK.

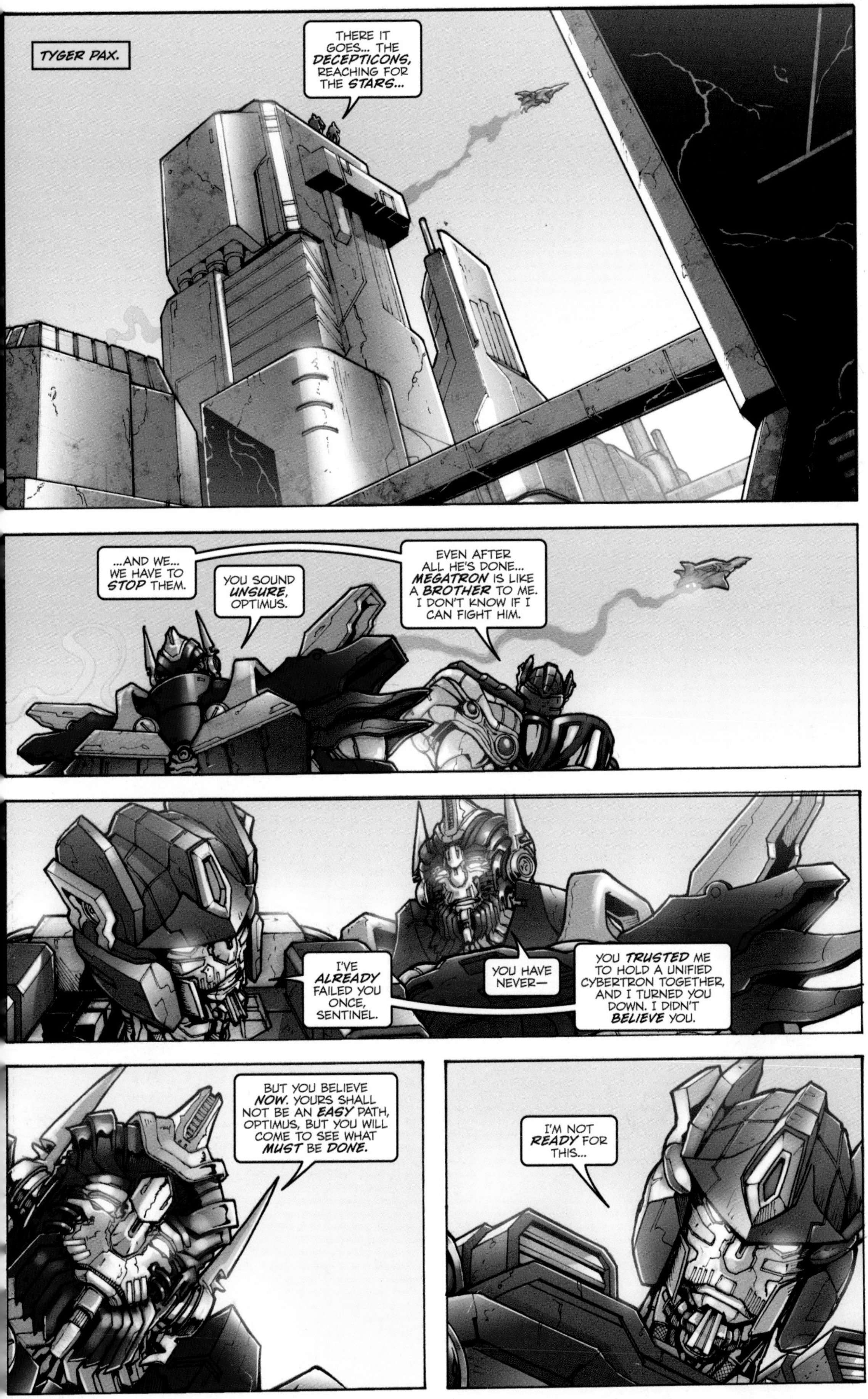
TYGER PAX.
THERE IT GOES... THE DECEPTICONS, REACHING FOR THE STARS...
...AND WE... WE HAVE TO STOP THEM.
YOU SOUND UNSURE, OPTIMUS.
EVEN AFTER ALL HE'S DONE... MEGATRON IS LIKE A BROTHER TO ME. I DON'T KNOW IF I CAN FIGHT HIM.
I'VE ALREADY FAILED YOU ONCE, SENTINEL.
YOU HAVE NEVER—
YOU TRUSTED ME TO HOLD A UNIFIED CYBERTRON TOGETHER, AND I TURNED YOU DOWN. I DIDN'T BELIEVE YOU.
BUT YOU BELIEVE NOW. YOURS SHALL NOT BE AN EASY PATH, OPTIMUS, BUT YOU WILL COME TO SEE WHAT MUST BE DONE.
I'M NOT READY FOR THIS...

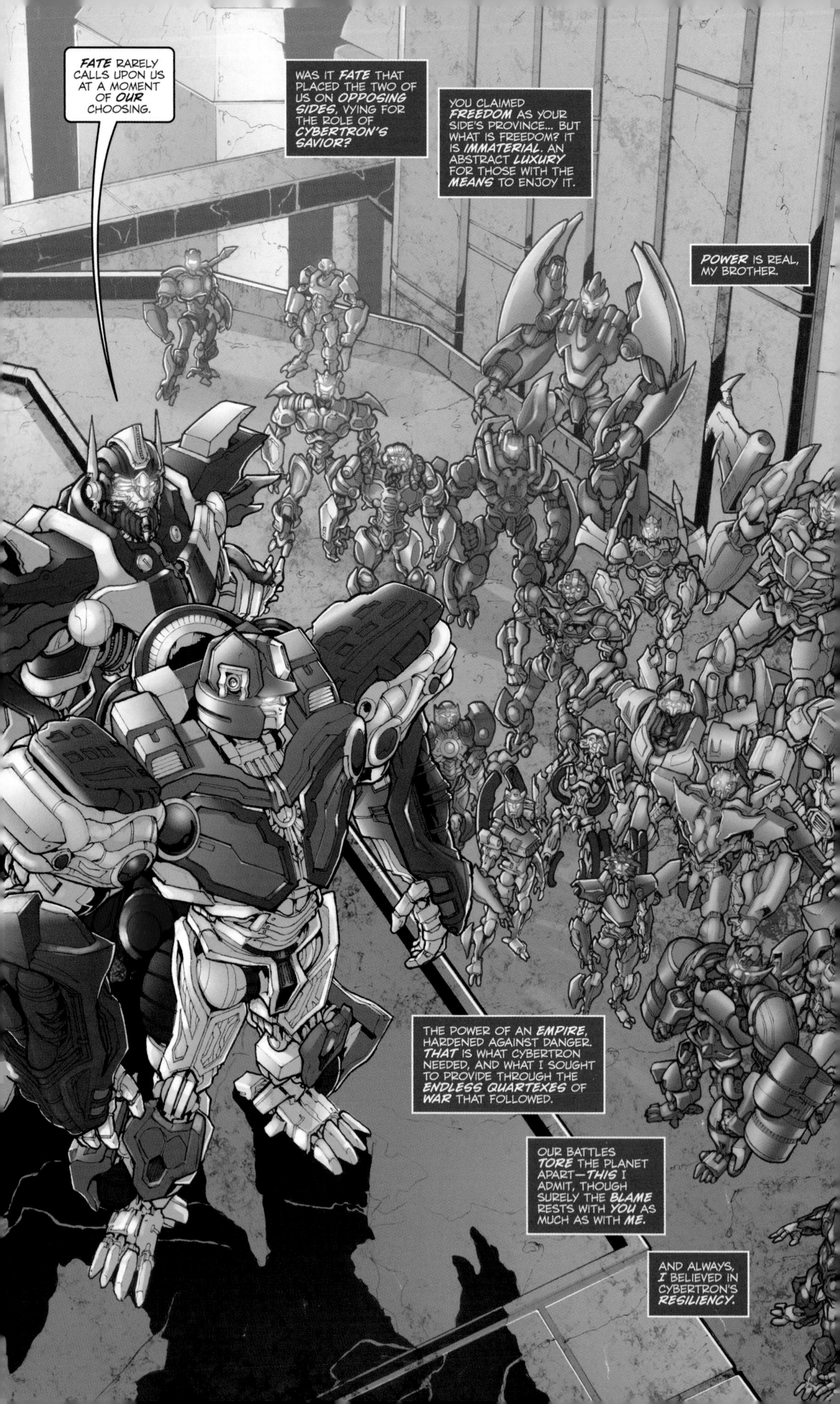

FATE RARELY CALLS UPON US AT A MOMENT OF OUR CHOOSING.
WAS IT FATE THAT PLACED THE TWO OF US ON OPPOSING SIDES, VYING FOR THE ROLE OF CYBERTRON'S SAVIOR?
YOU CLAIMED FREEDOM AS YOUR SIDE'S PROVINCE... BUT WHAT IS FREEDOM? IT IS IMMATERIAL. AN ABSTRACT LUXURY FOR THOSE WITH THE MEANS TO ENJOY IT.
POWER IS REAL, MY BROTHER.
THE POWER OF AN EMPIRE, HARDENED AGAINST DANGER. THAT IS WHAT CYBERTRON NEEDED, AND WHAT I SOUGHT TO PROVIDE THROUGH THE ENDLESS QUARTEXES OF WAR THAT FOLLOWED.
OUR BATTLES TORE THE PLANET APART—THIS I ADMIT, THOUGH SURELY THE BLAME RESTS WITH YOU AS MUCH AS WITH ME.
AND ALWAYS, I BELIEVED IN CYBERTRON'S RESILIENCY.

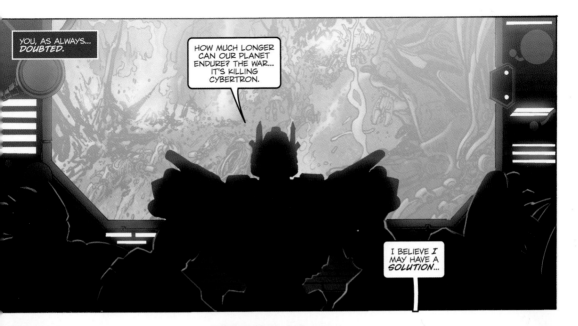

YOU, AS ALWAYS... *DOUBTED.*

HOW MUCH LONGER CAN OUR PLANET ENDURE? THE WAR... IT'S KILLING CYBERTRON.

I BELIEVE *I* MAY HAVE A *SOLUTION...*

...MY EXPERIMENTS HAVE COME TO *FRUITION.* I HAVE CREATED SOMETHING THAT WILL *GUARANTEE* AN END TO THIS WAR.

YOU MEAN WE'D BE ABLE TO *CRUSH* THE DECEPTICONS—*KILL* THE LOT OF 'EM?

IF *THAT* IS WHAT OUR LEADER *CHOOSES.*

NO. THAT'S THE METHOD OF OUR *ENEMY.* THERE *HAS* TO BE A WAY TO *WIN* WITHOUT RESORTING TO WHOLESALE *MURDER.*

YOU *CAN'T* BE SERIOUS! MEGATRON WOULDN'T *HESITATE* TO DESTROY *US!*

YOU CAME OVER TO *OUR* SIDE, IRONHIDE. YOU CHOSE *US* OVER MEGATRON. *WHY?*

BECAUSE WE'RE *BETTER* THAN HIM.

YOU'RE *RIGHT,* PRIME. IT'S NOT THE *AUTOBOT* WAY.

INDEED. MY INVENTION *DOES* PRESENT US WITH ANOTHER PATH TO VICTORY. OPTIMUS PRIME—

—YOUR *FOREFATHERS* WOULD BE *PROUD* OF *YOU.*

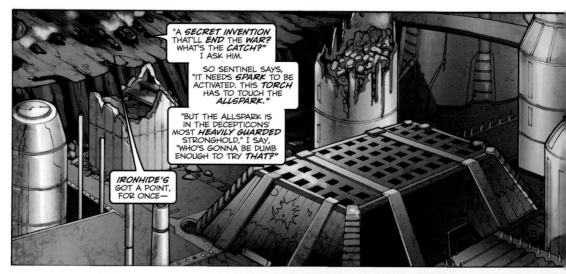

"A SECRET INVENTION THAT'LL END THE WAR? WHAT'S THE CATCH?" I ASK HIM.

SO SENTINEL SAYS, "IT NEEDS SPARK TO BE ACTIVATED. THIS TORCH HAS TO TOUCH THE ALLSPARK."

"BUT THE ALLSPARK IS IN THE DECEPTICONS' MOST HEAVILY GUARDED STRONGHOLD," I SAY, "WHO'S GONNA BE DUMB ENOUGH TO TRY THAT?"

IRONHIDE'S GOT A POINT, FOR ONCE—

HEY!

—THESE AREN'T TURBOFOXES WE'RE AFTER, ARCEE.

AND I'M NOT A HATCHLING, CHROMIA. I'VE LEARNED A THING OR TWO IN THIS WAR.

THERE IT IS—THE SIMFUR TEMPLE. HOME OF THE ALLSPARK.

ARCEE— SHE IS ONLY CONCERNED.

AND WHAT ABOUT YOU, ELITA?

I'M HONORED TO HAVE BOTH MY SISTERS WITH ME.

YOU THREE GET SENTINEL'S TORCH INSIDE, THE REST OF US'LL KEEP THE DECEPTICONS BUSY...

...FOR AS LONG AS WE CAN.

WHEN YOUR TRIBE *BUILT* THE TEMPLE, DID YOU IMAGINE YOU'D HAVE TO *BREAK IN*, OLD MAN?

HEH. AT LEAST I GET TO DO SOMETHING I'M *GOOD* AT.

NO ALARMS... *NOTHING*. WHY ISN'T ANYONE ATTACKING US?

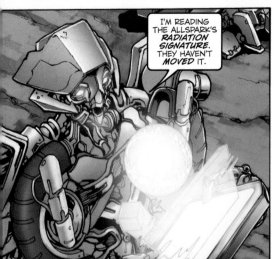

I'M READING THE ALLSPARK'S *RADIATION SIGNATURE*. THEY HAVEN'T *MOVED* IT.

VRRRRRRRR

WHAT'S *THAT*?

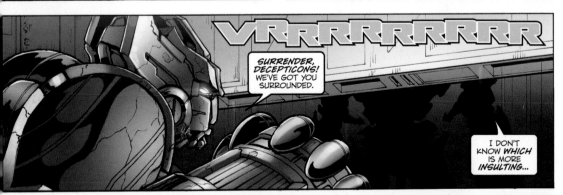

VRRRRRRRRR

SURRENDER, *DECEPTICONS!* WE'VE GOT YOU SURROUNDED.

I DON'T KNOW *WHICH* IS MORE *INSULTING*...

VRRRRRRRRR

...THAT YOU THOUGHT YOU COULD MAKE YOUR WAY TO *SIMFUR* WITHOUT MY AGENTS *FINDING OUT*...

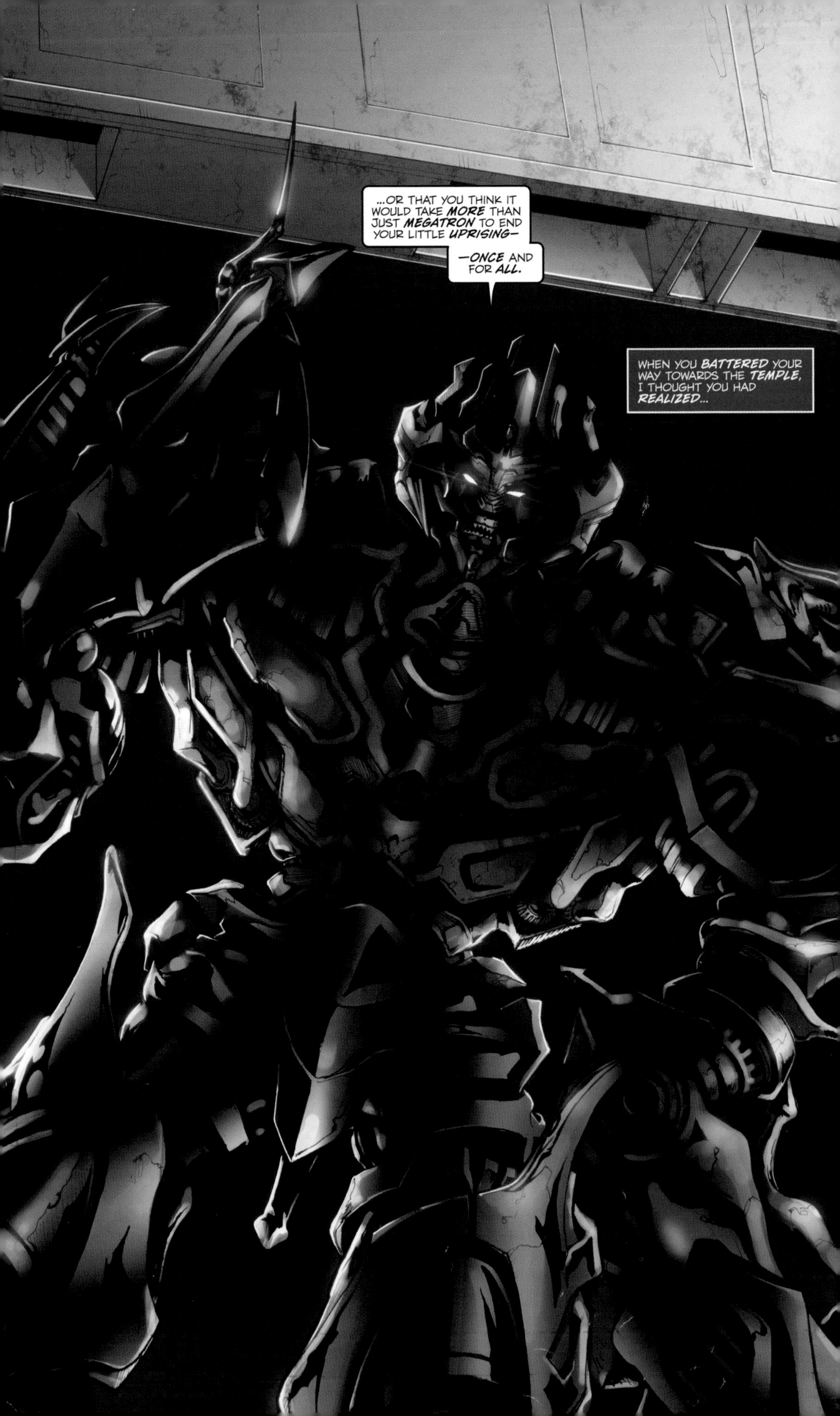
WHEN YOU BATTERED YOUR WAY TOWARDS THE TEMPLE, I THOUGHT YOU HAD REALIZED...
...OR THAT YOU THINK IT WOULD TAKE MORE THAN JUST MEGATRON TO END YOUR LITTLE UPRISING—
—ONCE AND FOR ALL.

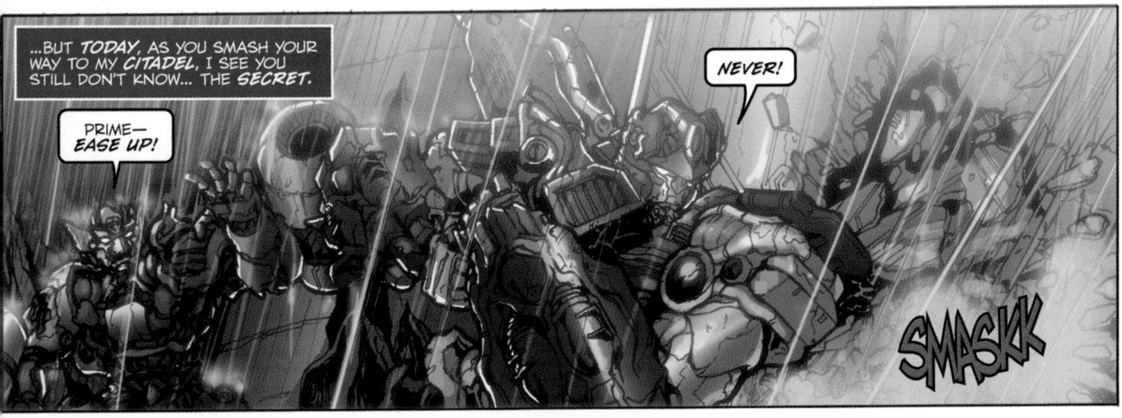
...BUT TODAY, AS YOU SMASH YOUR WAY TO MY CITADEL, I SEE YOU STILL DON'T KNOW... THE SECRET.
PRIME— EASE UP!
NEVER!
SMASKK

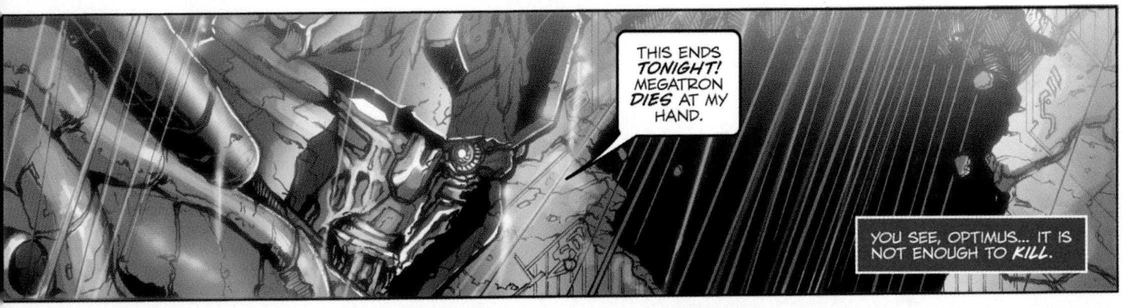
THIS ENDS TONIGHT! MEGATRON DIES AT MY HAND.
YOU SEE, OPTIMUS... IT IS NOT ENOUGH TO KILL.

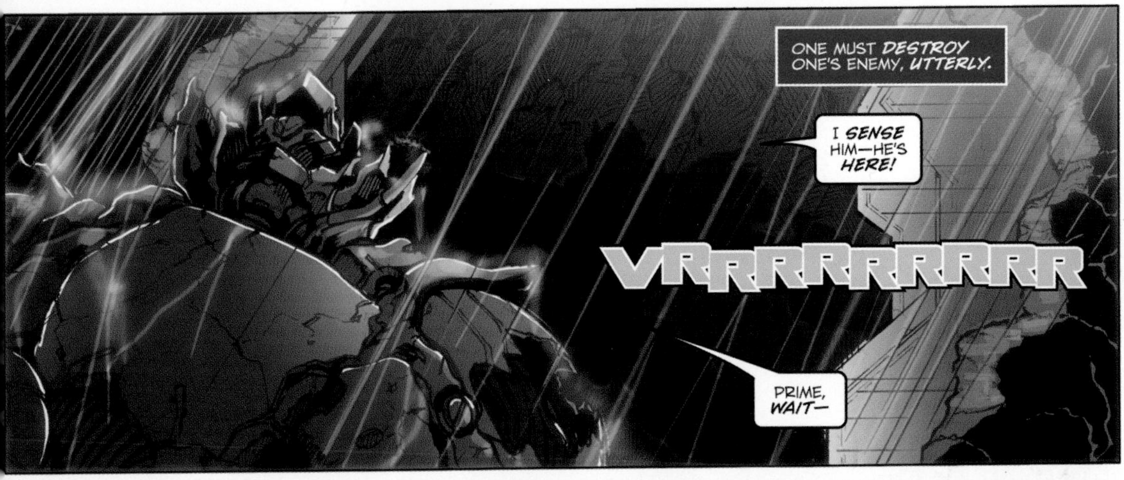
ONE MUST DESTROY ONE'S ENEMY, UTTERLY.
I SENSE HIM—HE'S HERE!
VRRRRRRRRRR
PRIME, WAIT—

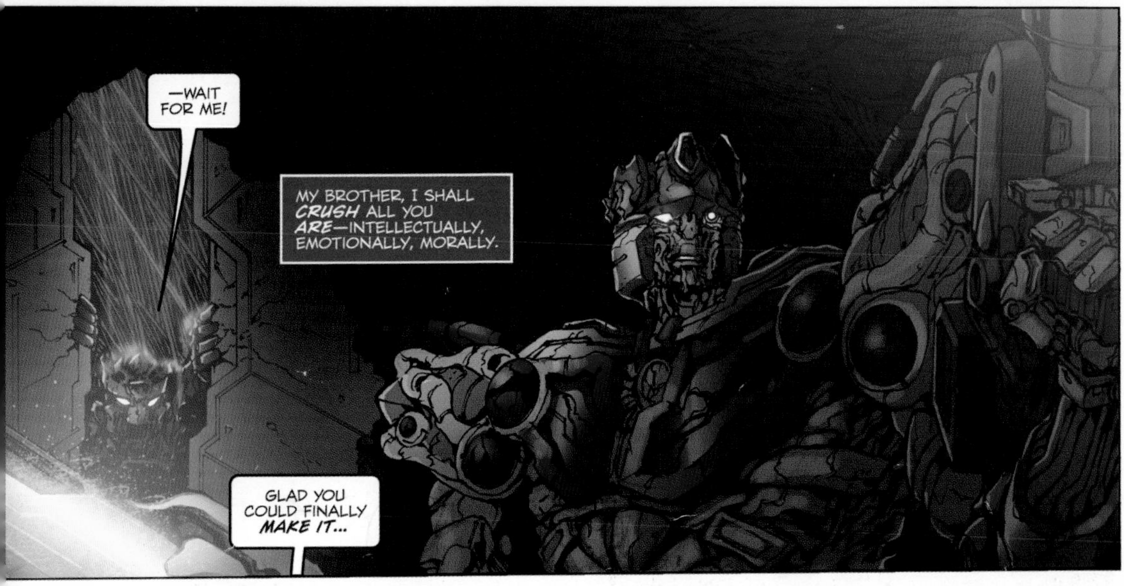
—WAIT FOR ME!
MY BROTHER, I SHALL CRUSH ALL YOU ARE—INTELLECTUALLY, EMOTIONALLY, MORALLY.
GLAD YOU COULD FINALLY MAKE IT...

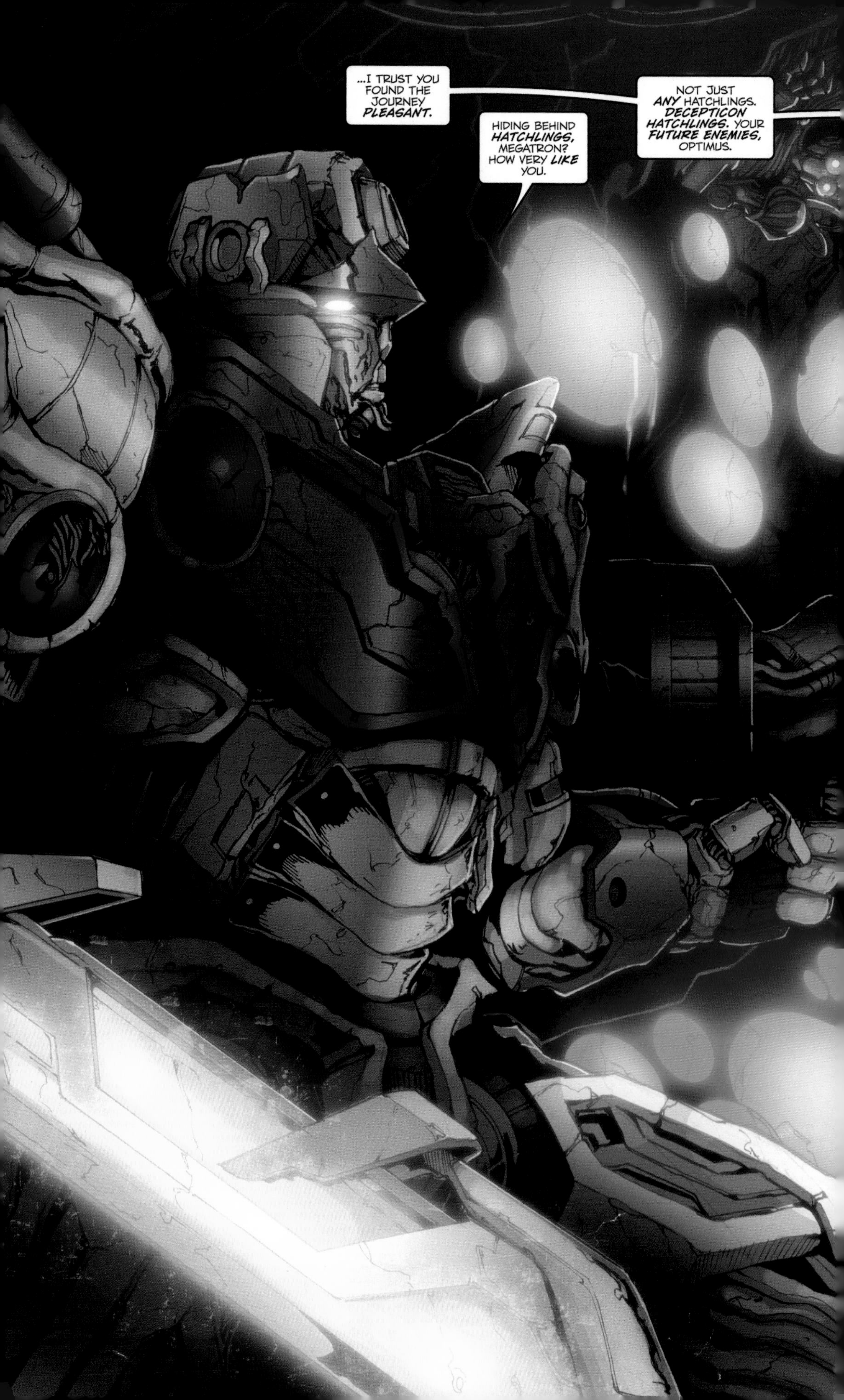
...I TRUST YOU FOUND THE JOURNEY PLEASANT.
HIDING BEHIND HATCHLINGS, MEGATRON? HOW VERY LIKE YOU.
NOT JUST ANY HATCHLINGS. DECEPTICON HATCHLINGS. YOUR FUTURE ENEMIES, OPTIMUS.

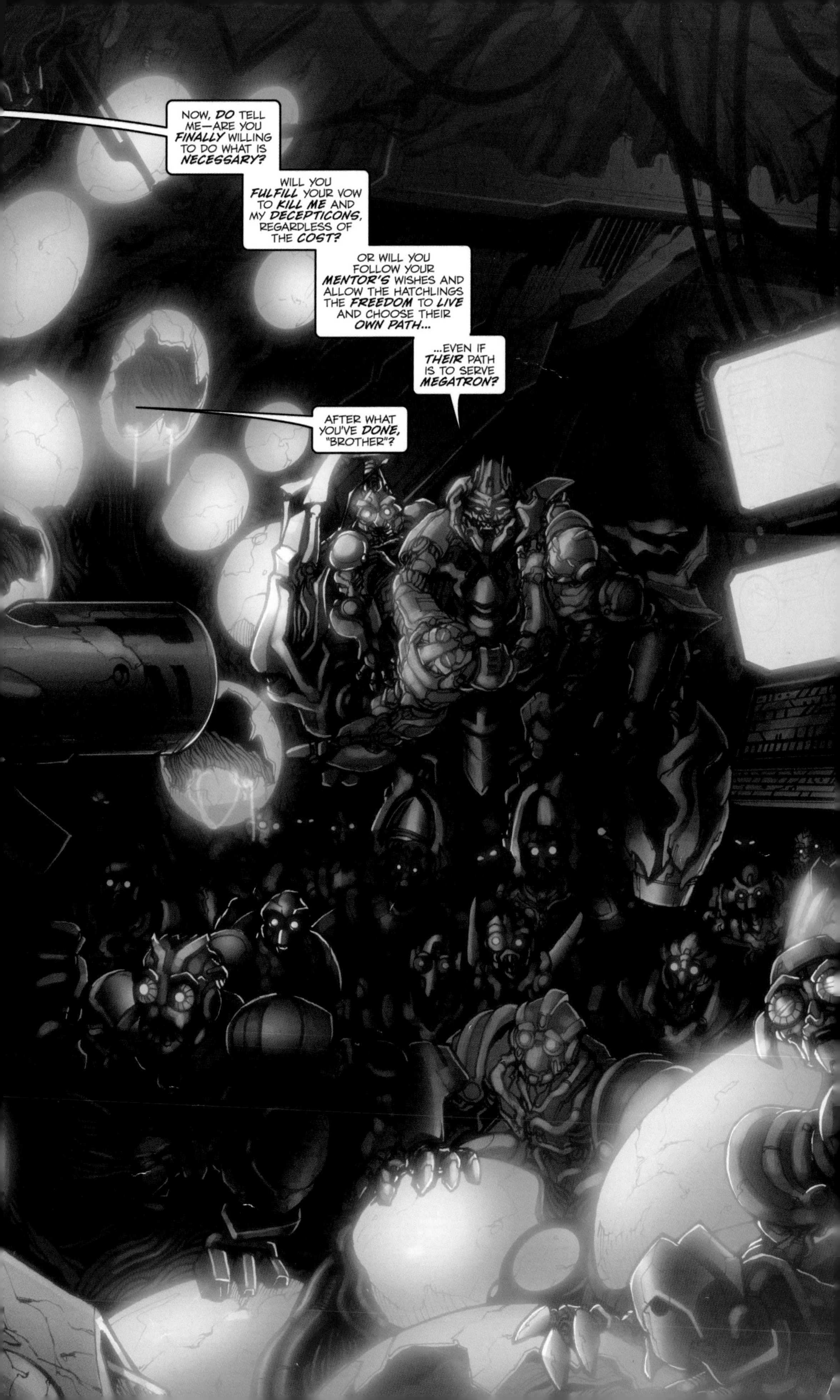
NOW, DO TELL ME—ARE YOU FINALLY WILLING TO DO WHAT IS NECESSARY?
WILL YOU FULFILL YOUR VOW TO KILL ME AND MY DECEPTICONS, REGARDLESS OF THE COST?
OR WILL YOU FOLLOW YOUR MENTOR'S WISHES AND ALLOW THE HATCHLINGS THE FREEDOM TO LIVE AND CHOOSE THEIR OWN PATH...
...EVEN IF THEIR PATH IS TO SERVE MEGATRON?
AFTER WHAT YOU'VE DONE, "BROTHER"?

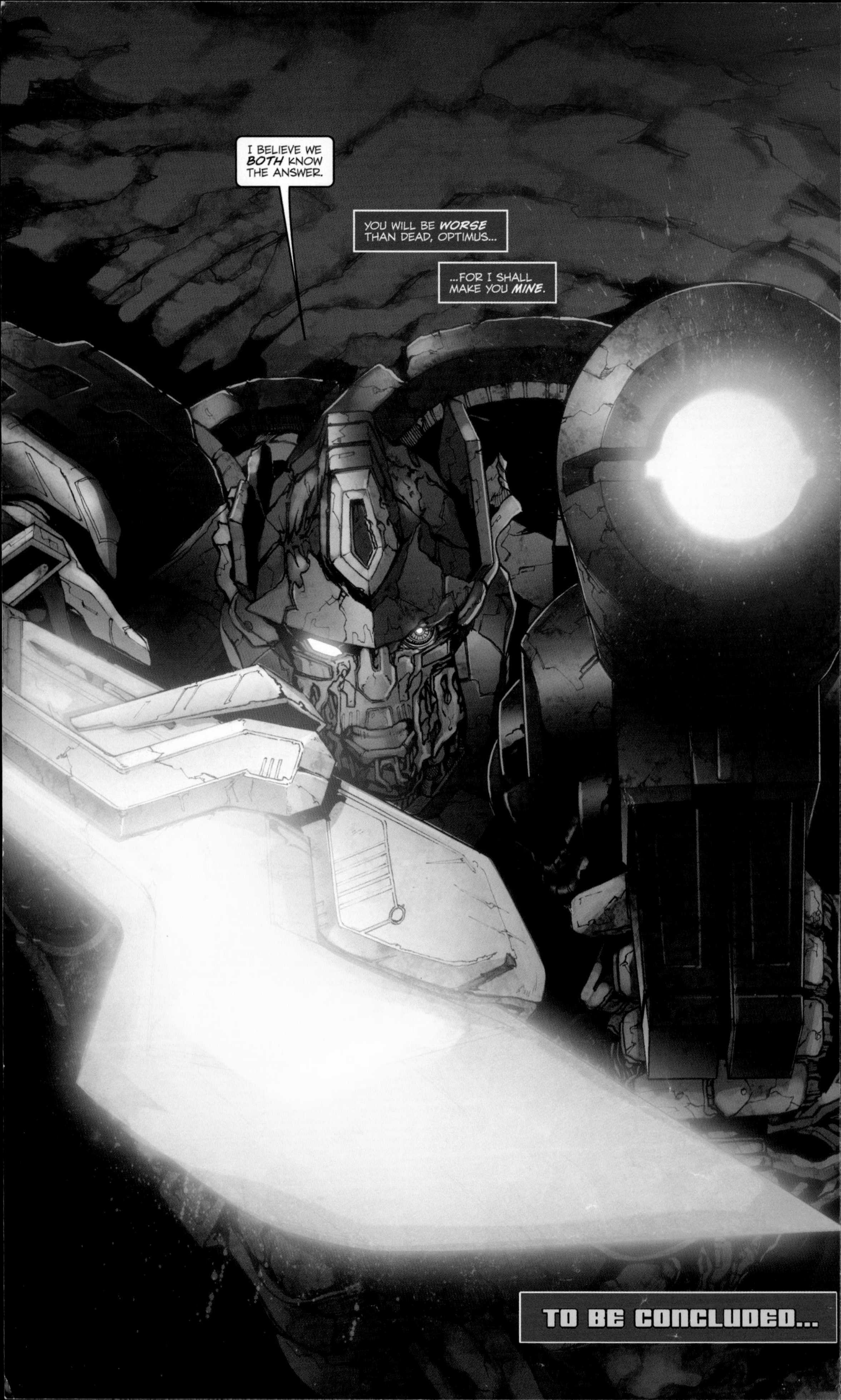
I BELIEVE WE BOTH KNOW THE ANSWER.
YOU WILL BE WORSE THAN DEAD, OPTIMUS...
...FOR I SHALL MAKE YOU MINE.
TO BE CONCLUDED...